NOT QUITE MOTHER'S DAY

A story about Mothering Sunday

Written by Jenny Gubb

Pictures by Jane Fox

The National Society/Church House Publishing
Church House, Great Smith Street, London SW1P 3NZ

ISBN 0 7151 4798 6

Published 1990 jointly by The National Society and Church House Publishing

Printed in Great Britain by The Ludo Press Ltd, London SW18 3DG

It was Mothering Sunday. Victoria Simmonds' mother
was cross with her. And when her mother was cross with
her, Victoria Simmonds pretended that her mother was
not her real mother at all.

She pretended instead
that her mother was a
wicked old witch.

Sometimes, when her mother was cross with her, Victoria Simmonds pretended that her REAL mother was a queen and that she was REALLY a princess, with jewels and silk dresses.

Her mother, the queen, would be very gracious and give her jam tarts and honey sandwiches every day for tea. Everyone would be very nice to Victoria Simmonds and give her everything she wanted, because she was a princess.

Sometimes, when her mother was cross with her, Victoria Simmonds pretended that her REAL mother was a famous mountaineer. Then all the children at school would come and ask her which mountain her mother was conquering at the moment. She would be very casual and just say 'K2' or 'Ben Nevis'. And everyone would look it up on the map and Mrs Penfold would let them do a project on it.

Her mother would be in all the newspapers. And everyone would be very nice to Victoria Simmonds and give her everything she wanted, because she was the daughter of a famous mountaineer.

Sometimes, when her mother was cross with her, Victoria Simmonds pretended that her REAL mother was a proper mother, like they have on television. Then everyone would say her mother was a saint because she smiled all the time, and her whites were always very white, and her Yorkshire puddings always rose, and her hands were always as soft as her beautiful voice.

And everyone would be very nice to Victoria Simmonds and give her everything she wanted, because she had such a perfectly saintly mother.

But then Victoria Simmonds began to think.

She thought that if her mother were really a queen, she would hardly ever see her, because she would always be touring the Commonwealth and opening Parliament and Trooping the Colour.

And then she thought that if her mother were really a mountaineer, she would hardly ever see her, because she would always be testing her crampons and coiling her ropes and planning routes up the north face.

And then she thought that if her mother were really a proper mother like they have on television, she would hardly ever see her because she would always be hoovering and cleaning the windows and making complicated puddings for tea.

Victoria Simmonds thought again.

If her mother were REALLY a queen, she wouldn't take her to the Little Chef for fish fingers and chips, and she wouldn't put on her wellies to collect frog spawn in a jar.

If her mother were REALLY a famous mountaineer,
she wouldn't want to play in the sand pit in the park.

And if her mother were REALLY a proper mother
like they have on television, she wouldn't let her do
her cutting and sticking in the dining room.

On the whole and all things considered, Victoria Simmonds decided that even though her mother was sometimes cross with her, she was still the best mother in the whole wide world.

And to show how much she loved her, she went out into the garden and picked every single daffodil as a present for Mothering Sunday.